DINOSAUR BEACH

by Liza Donnelly

SCHOLASTIC INC./New York

For Michael

A LUCAS • EVANS BOOK

LIBRARY OF CONGRESS
Library of Congress Cataloging-in-Publication Data
Donnelly, Liza.
Dinosaur beach / by Liza Donnelly.
p.   cm.
Summary: Frightened sunbathers flee from a crowded beach when someone
yells, "Shark!"; but it's really a friendly elasmosaurus who then takes
our boy hero to Dinosaur Beach.
ISBN 0-590-42175-1
[1. Dinosaurs — Fiction.] I. Title.
PZ7.D7195Dg 1989   [E] — dc19   88-12209   CIP   AC
12 11 10 9 8 7 6 5 4 3 2 1   9/8 0 1 2 3 4/9
Printed in the U.S.A.   36

First Scholastic printing, May 1989

PRESENTED BY

Chase Singeton

1990

"Wake up, Bones! Let's go to the beach!"

"Did you know that some dinosaurs lived in the sea?"

"It must have been great back then.
Think of it — dinosaurs on the beach!"

"I'll show you what one looked like."

"They were very, very big . . . "

" . . . and probably very friendly."

"Bones, could it be?"

"It looks like . . . "

" . . . an elasmosaurus!"

*"Hop on!"

"I wonder where he's taking us."

"WOW!!!"

"See? They are friendly."

"And they're fun, too!"

* "Follow me."

"C'mon, Bones. . . ."

"LOOK . . .

. . . it's you and me!"

* "Time to go, my friends."

"Good-bye! Thank you."

"There they are! What happened?"

"We rode on a dinosaur to Dinosaur Beach!"

"There was a diplodocus and a tylosaurus
and a phobosuchus and — "

"Nutty kid!"

" — and a very friendly elasmosaurus!"

GLOSSARY

ARCHELON (ARK-uh-lon) Not a dinosaur, but a giant turtle that was 12 feet long. Archelon (ruler tortoise) ate fish and laid its eggs on the beach.

COELOPHYSIS (SEE-lo-fehz-iss) This dinosaur was light and quick on its feet. It had a long body, but was only three feet high at the hips. Coelophysis probably lived in family groups.

DIPLODOCUS (dih-PLOD-uh-kuss) This plant eater was probably the largest dinosaur, measuring 90 feet long. It lived in swamps and used its enormous tail for defense.

ELASMOSAURUS (eh-laz-muh-SAWR-us) This marine reptile was not a dinosaur, but lived during the same time. A fish eater, it was 43 feet long and very streamlined. It moved slowly through the ocean, propelled by narrow flippers.

EUPARKERIA (you-par-KEER-ee-uh) This ancient reptile ran swiftly on two hind legs, but spent most of its time walking on all four. It had armoured plates on its back, was only five feet long, and weighed 40 pounds.

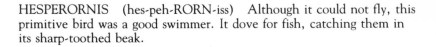

HESPERORNIS (hes-peh-RORN-iss) Although it could not fly, this primitive bird was a good swimmer. It dove for fish, catching them in its sharp-toothed beak.

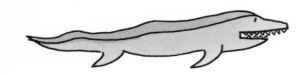

MOSASAURUS (MO-zuh-sawr-us) Not a dinosaur, but a seagoing lizard. Twenty to 50 feet long, it had a huge jaw filled with teeth. Mosasaurus probably ate small sea animals.

PENTACERATOPS (pen-tah-SAIR-uh-tops) This dinosaur had an enormous neck shield with frills and five horns on its head. It was 20 feet long and ate plants.

PHOBOSUCHUS (fo-bo-SOOK-us) No a dinosaur but the largest crocodile that eve lived. Phobosuchus (fear crocodile) was a 5 foot-long meat eater, and probably preyed on anything it could catch.

RHAMPHORHYNCHUS (ram-fo-RINK-us) Like other pterosaurs (winged lizards) this one had a small body (only 18 inches!) and large wings. It would catch fish in flight by scooping them out of the water with its toothed beak.

TYLOSAURUS (tye-lah-SAWR-us) Not a dinosaur, but a mosasaurus (seagoing lizard), this slim creature was 20 to 40 feet long. It had a huge jaw and ate fish and shellfish.